This Walker
book belongs to:

_____

_____

_____

For Ossie

First published 2015 by Walker Books Ltd, 87 Vauxhall Walk, London SE11 5HJ
This edition published 2016 • 1 2 3 4 5 6 7 8 9 10 • © 2015 Daisy Hirst • The right
of Daisy Hirst to be identified as author and illustrator of
this work has been asserted by her in accordance
with the Copyright, Designs and Patents Act
1988 • This book has been typeset in Stempel
Schneidler • Printed in China • All rights
reserved. No part of this book may be
reproduced, transmitted or stored in
an information retrieval system in
any form or by any means, graphic,
electronic or mechanical, including
photocopying, taping and recording,
without prior written permission
from the publisher. • British
Library Cataloguing in Publication
Data: a catalogue record for this
book is available from the British
Library • ISBN 978-1-4063-6552-8

www.walker.co.uk

The Girl with the Parrot on her Head

Daisy Hirst

WALKER BOOKS
AND SUBSIDIARIES

LONDON · BOSTON · SYDNEY · AUCKLAND

Once there was a girl with
a parrot on her head.

Her name was Isabel,
and she had a friend
called Simon

who was very good with newts.

But one day Simon
went away in a truck

and he never
came back.

For a while Isabel
hated everything.

The parrot
went to sit
on top of the
wardrobe.

Until Isabel felt quiet inside, and
decided to like being on her own.

The girl with the parrot on her head did not need friends.

She had the parrot on her head, and ...

CASTLES

CARS

HATS

BEARS

MONSTER

THE DARK

she had a **system**.

She sorted things out with the help
of the parrot, and pushed all the boxes
to the corner of her room.

Sometimes, at night, the parrot felt worried
about the boxes, especially the box of wolves.

"Pah!" said the girl with the parrot on her
head. "Don't be such a scaredy-parrot."

But secretly she was worried too –
she thought that one of the wolves
might be too big for the system.

So when she
found the biggest box
she'd ever seen, the girl with
the parrot on her head called out,
"Aha! This box is perfect for the wolf."

However,
something
was already inside.

"Oh," said Isabel.
"Is this your box?"

"Sort of," said the boy. "I was going to use it for a den."

"Why not a castle?" asked Isabel. "Why not an ostrich farm? Or a space station next to the moon?"

"No reason," said the boy, whose name was Chester. "But what did you need it for?"

Isabel explained about the wolf.

"You can't keep a wolf in a cardboard box!" said Chester. "They're supposed to live in forests far away."

"Oh," said Isabel. "Well, could you please help me tell the wolf to go?"

Isabel and Chester told the wolf
about the forests, great plains and
mountains far away, where a wolf
could run and stop to howl and
run again all day and night.

The wolf left at once.

"So," said Chester.
"How about this box?"

The girl with the parrot on her head liked being on her own, but Chester had a way with umbrellas and sticky tape

and Isabel knew where to find martians and helmets and string …

and the space station
really needed *two*
astronauts

and a parrot with a teacup on its head.

By the same author:

ISBN 978-1-4063-5431-7